G.I. JOE
THE RISE OF COBRA

NINJA SHOWDOWN!

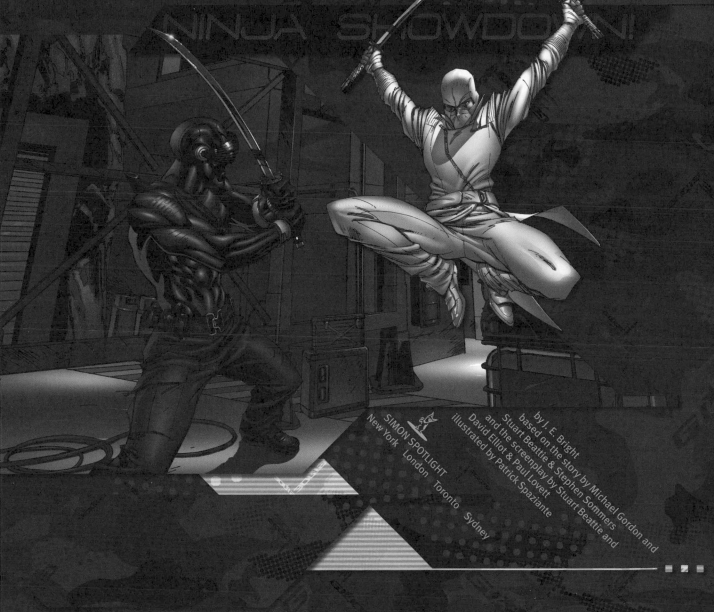

by J. E. Bright
based on the story by Michael Gordon and
Stuart Beattie & Stephen Sommers
and the screenplay by Stuart Beattie and
David Elliot & Paul Lovett
illustrated by Patrick Spaziante

SIMON SPOTLIGHT
New York   London   Toronto   Sydney

An imprint of Simon & Schuster Children's Publishing Division
1230 Avenue of the Americas, New York, New York 10020

SIMON SPOTLIGHT

Based on Hasbro's G.I. JOE® Characters

HASBRO and its logo, GI JOE and all related characters are trademarks of
Hasbro and are used with permission. © 2009 Hasbro. All Rights Reserved.
© 2009 Paramount Pictures Corporation. All Rights Reserved.

SIMON SPOTLIGHT and colophon are registered trademarks of Simon & Schuster, Inc.

Manufactured in the United States of America
First Edition 1 2 3 4 5 6 7 8 9 10
ISBN: 978-1-4169-7882-4

The G.I. JOE base, the Pit, was under attack!

Snake Eyes—G.I. JOE's skilled ninja—sprang to his feet to defend his base. The criminals had come back to get what they weren't able to steal the last time: a very dangerous case of weapons. But as he battled, Snake Eyes was shocked to cross swords with another very skilled ninja . . . a villain who had a familiar Arishikage clan marking on his arm.

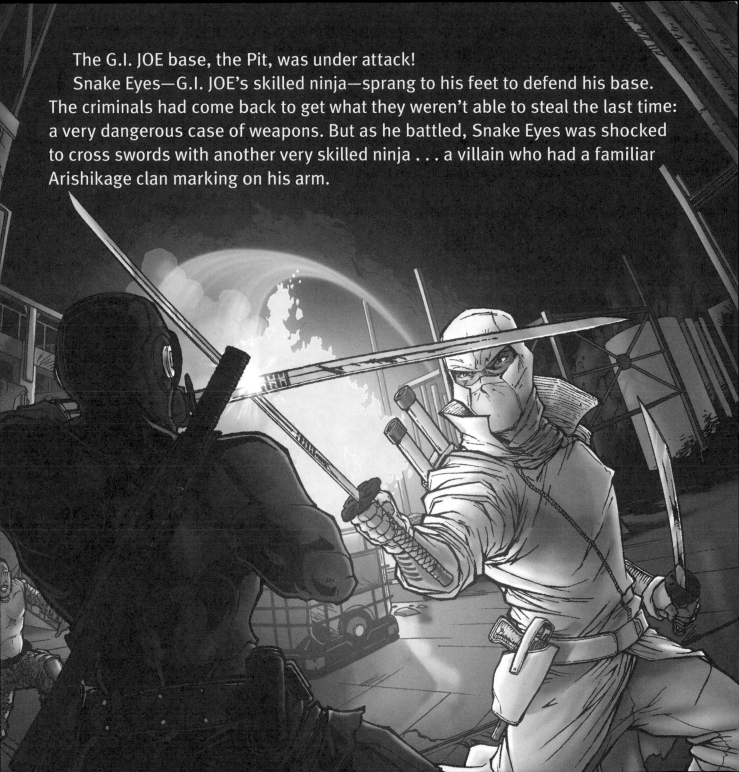

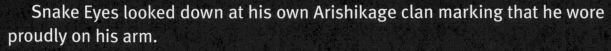

Snake Eyes looked down at his own Arishikage clan marking that he wore proudly on his arm.

"Hello, *brother*," the ninja villain said, sneering at Snake Eyes.

Snake Eyes knew the voice immediately—it was Storm Shadow! This villain was Snake Eyes's archenemy, and the reason he had taken a vow of silence so long ago. There was a lifetime of bad blood between the two men.

The two ninjas fought fiercely. Storm Shadow elbowed Snake Eyes in the face, knocking him down. Before Snake Eyes could react, Storm Shadow and his fellow criminals used their Jetpacks to escape the Pit—with the case of dangerous weapons in hand!

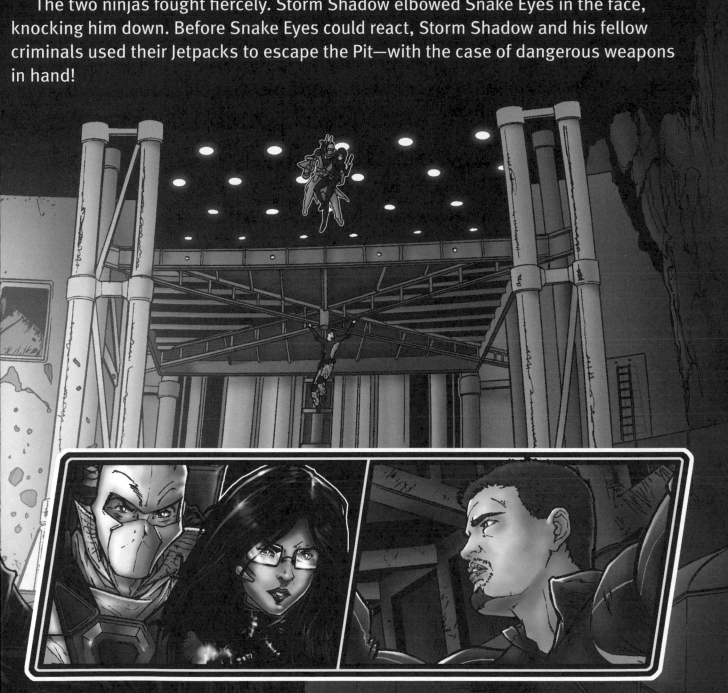

Snake Eyes was furious! He couldn't believe Storm Shadow had won again. He remembered back to when they first met. Snake Eyes was a ten-year-old American orphan living alone on the streets of Tokyo, Japan. One rainy night he was wandering outside a temple, searching for food. Suddenly he noticed a light in the kitchen window, and set his eyes on a large pot on the stove. He was so hungry that he snuck in.

Just as he took his first bite of warm, delicious rice, he was startled by screaming.

"Thief!" shouted a young Storm Shadow. The red clan markings on his forearm were clearly visible.

Snake Eyes looked at the young, healthy, well-fed boy, and anger rose up inside him. Could this boy not spare a bowl of rice? Storm Shadow attacked, and suddenly the two boys were fighting wildly, with knives, pots, pans, and forks—breaking everything in the kitchen. Snake Eyes had street-fighting skills, but Storm Shadow had ninja training.

Storm Shadow pinned Snake Eyes down on the floor, shoving his foot into the space between Snake Eyes's neck and back.

"Storm Shadow!" the Master yelled. "Enough!"

"He was stealing, Father," Storm Shadow said. "He is a thief, and a weakling."

"He doesn't fight like a weakling," replied the Master.

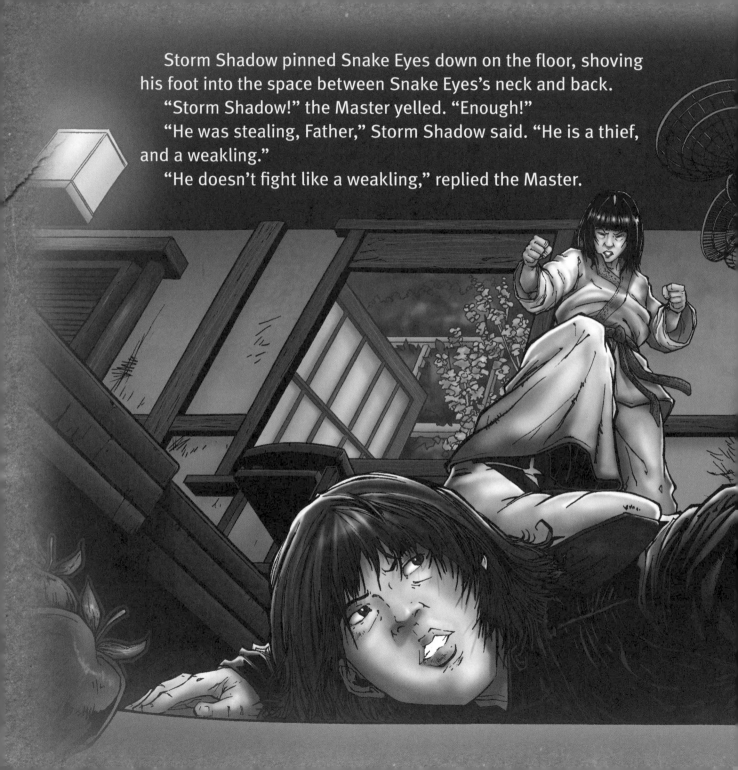

The Master was impressed by the orphan's fierce glare and survival skills. He gave him the name Snake Eyes and adopted him for training in the temple.

The Master taught Snake Eyes all of his ninja skills and secrets. More important than his training, the Master loved and nurtured Snake Eyes, raising him as Storm Shadow's brother—as a son.

Though their history went back many years, the anger Snake Eyes and Storm Shadow felt toward each other was as fresh as it was on the day they met. Snake Eyes would not let Storm Shadow win the next time. He and his team would track the villains down, and Storm Shadow would finally pay for the damage he'd done.

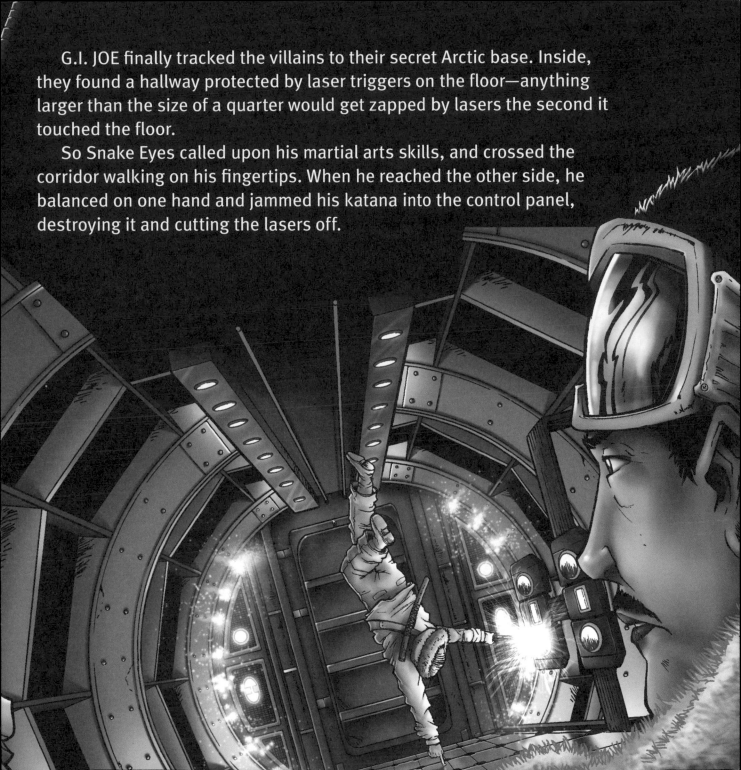

G.I. JOE finally tracked the villains to their secret Arctic base. Inside, they found a hallway protected by laser triggers on the floor—anything larger than the size of a quarter would get zapped by lasers the second it touched the floor.

So Snake Eyes called upon his martial arts skills, and crossed the corridor walking on his fingertips. When he reached the other side, he balanced on one hand and jammed his katana into the control panel, destroying it and cutting the lasers off.

Once they were inside the base, the team found the control room. Snake Eyes shut off the powerful pulse cannon protecting the base from the G.I. JOE submarine that was waiting in the ocean outside.

In a sneak attack, Storm Shadow appeared and sliced Snake Eyes's arm. Then the villain turned the cannon back on. But Snake Eyes would not back down. He leaped at his sword brother, and the battle began!

Snake Eyes remembered practicing sword fighting with Storm Shadow when they were ten-year-olds at the Arishikage temple. Even though Storm Shadow won all the practice battles, the Master was not impressed.

Years later, the two fully grown Arishikage ninjas were still fighting, only this time the Master wasn't there to see who would win. They fought fiercely in the control room, then tumbled down a long shaft onto a platform inches above the freezing Arctic water . . . in the space where the pulse cannon's lasers charged up!

Lasers sizzled across the platform as the cannon prepared to fire at the G.I. JOE submarine. Snake Eyes and Storm Shadow continued to fight, reflecting the burning beams with their blades, until Storm Shadow kicked Snake Eyes and he lost his grip on his katana!

Once again, Snake Eyes found his mind wandering back to another childhood memory: the first time he defeated Storm Shadow in battle.

Snake Eyes had sidestepped Storm Shadow's charge, and flipped Storm Shadow's arm around. Then Snake Eyes had pointed his sword at Storm Shadow's eye.

The Master had clapped in approval. He had been so proud of Snake Eyes. Storm Shadow had been shocked—his father had never once clapped when he'd won! Slapping Snake Eyes's sword to the side, Storm Shadow had stalked away furiously.

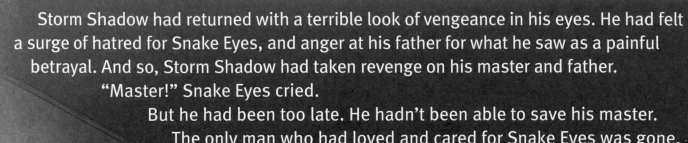

Storm Shadow had returned with a terrible look of vengeance in his eyes. He had felt a surge of hatred for Snake Eyes, and anger at his father for what he saw as a painful betrayal. And so, Storm Shadow had taken revenge on his master and father.

"Master!" Snake Eyes cried.

But he had been too late. He hadn't been able to save his master. The only man who had loved and cared for Snake Eyes was gone, forever, at the hands of Storm Shadow.

But Snake Eyes had been too late, once again. Storm Shadow had escaped over the temple roof, disappearing into the darkness.

From that point forward, Snake Eyes had sworn to never speak another word until he had punished Storm Shadow for his terrible betrayal.

The pulse cannon fired, ripping Snake Eyes from his daydream and forcing him back into reality. The base's lasers fizzled out, recharging. Storm Shadow kicked the katana over to Snake Eyes, ready to resume their battle.

"You took a vow of silence to avenge our master," said Storm Shadow. "But now you will go without a word."

The laser grid blazed on again, surprising Storm Shadow and throwing him back. Snake Eyes caught his sword brother with his legs, holding him up as the lasers reignited.

Suddenly one of the lasers flashed across Storm Shadow's neck and he screamed in pain. Then without warning, Storm Shadow toppled backward off the platform . . . falling down into the freezing water below.

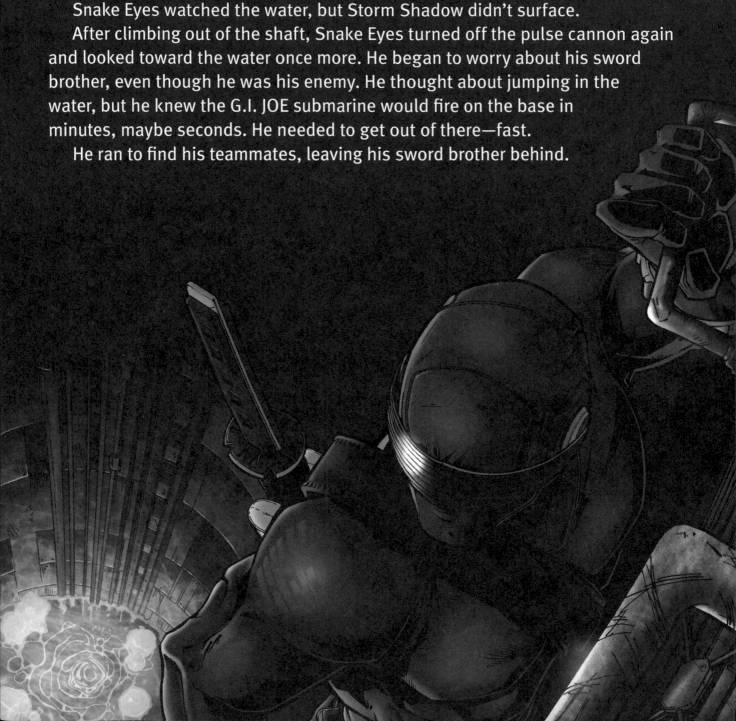

Snake Eyes watched the water, but Storm Shadow didn't surface.

After climbing out of the shaft, Snake Eyes turned off the pulse cannon again and looked toward the water once more. He began to worry about his sword brother, even though he was his enemy. He thought about jumping in the water, but he knew the G.I. JOE submarine would fire on the base in minutes, maybe seconds. He needed to get out of there—fast.

He ran to find his teammates, leaving his sword brother behind.

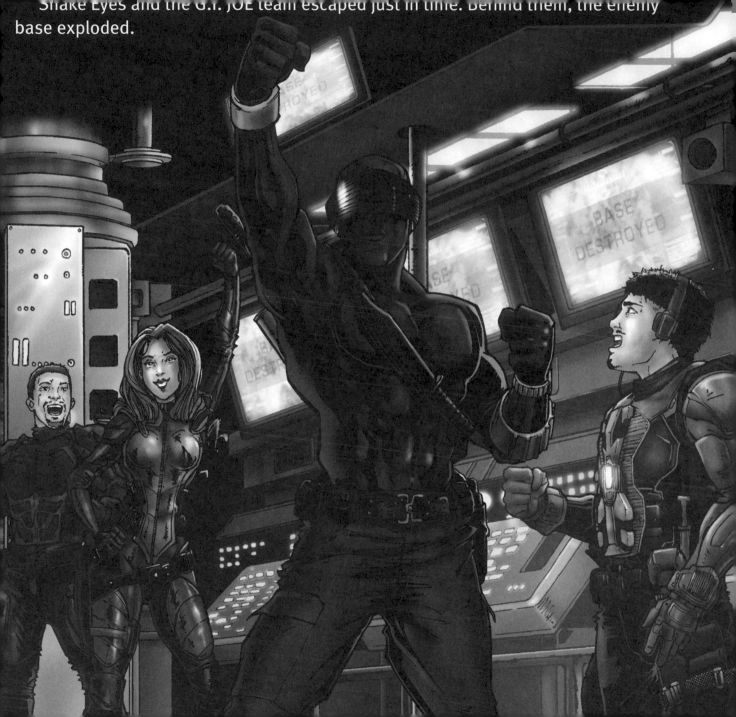

Shake Eyes and the G.I. JOE team escaped just in time. Behind them, the enemy base exploded.

Back at the Pit, G.I. JOE celebrated their victory.

Snake Eyes was happy the team got the dangerous weapons case back to the Pit safely. But he couldn't stop thinking about his archenemy. He hoped Storm Shadow escaped somehow . . . so that one day his beloved master would be truly avenged.

He had a feeling their lifelong battle was far from over.

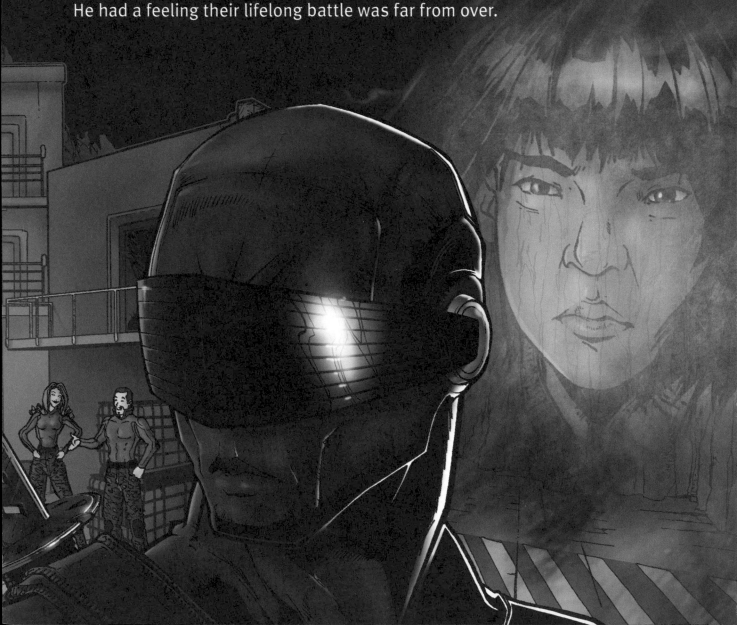